CW00918991

Published by Ladybird Books Ltd
27 Wrights Lane London W8 5TZ
A Penguin Company
2 4 6 8 10 9 7 5 3 1

LADYBIRD and the device of a Ladybird are trademarks of Ladybird Books Ltd

Printed in Italy

Next Stop... DigiWorld!

Ladybird

Matt, Izzy, Mimi, T.K., Sora, Tai and
Joe were at summer camp having fun.

Then suddenly the weather started to do really weird things.

Even though it was the middle of summer, it started snowing!

Then strange lights filled the sky.
The friends moved closer.

Suddenly, beams
of light shot up
from the ground
at their feet.

"Look!" said Mimi. "I can see something inside each one."

But at that very moment, they were all whisked up into the air and found themselves hurtling through space...

Finally, they landed on the ground with a bump. They had been transported to a mysterious new world...

...and there was a cool little monster waiting for each of them! "Welcome to DigiWorld!" the monsters cried.

MOTIMON

"We're Digital Monsters. We want to be your friends!" said the Digimons.

TANEMON

KOROMON

YOKOMON

TSUNOMON

BUKAMON

TOKOMON

But before they could all get to know each other better, they heard a terrible buzzing noise.

"Watch out!" cried Motimon. "That's Kuwagamon! He's an evil Digimon."

Quickly, the Digimons led
the friends to a special
place called a hiding tree.

They hid for ages, but Kuwagamon was ready for them – just as soon as they stepped out of the tree.

Just as they gave up hope,
the Digimons surrounded
Kuwagamon and something
amazing happened...

PATAMON

GOMAMON

BIYOMON

AGUMON

...the Digimons became bigger and bigger, and stronger and stronger.

TENTOMON

GABUMON

PALMON

They had amazing powers and looked really scary – they had digivolved!

Kuwagamon was no match for the Digimons' new powers. He was beaten.

The gang knew that the Digimons
were really special friends. "You guys
are too cool for words!" said Matt.

Matt, Izzy, Mimi, T.K., Sora, Tai and Joe didn't know how long it would take them to find their way home, but they knew that with their Digimons, they made an unbeatable team.